DATE DUE

G
c.1

Gangloff, Deborah
Albert & Victoria

Albert
&
Victoria

Albert & Victoria

a novel by
Deborah Gangloff
with pictures by
Bill Woodman

Crown Publishers, Inc.
New York

With special thanks to Brooke

Library of Congress Cataloging-in-Publication Data
Gangloff, Deborah. Albert & Victoria/by Deborah Gangloff.
Summary: Two best friends, Albert and Victoria, enjoy a very
pleasant life in the walls of the sixty-eighth floor of the Empire State
Building until Victoria decides not to hibernate for the winter like the
rest of the bugs. [1. Insects—Fiction. 2. Friendship—Fiction.]
I. Title. PZ7.G147A1 1989 [Fic]—dc19

ISBN 0-517-57044-0

10 9 8 7 6 5 4 3 2 1

First Edition

For My Parents

VICTORIA   ALBERT

Author's Note
The Albert and Victoria depicted
in these pages should not be confused with
the more famous Victoria and Albert, who were
of an earlier time, of another continent,
and of an entirely different
species.

ALBERT   VICTORIA

prologue

If you were to think of something "tall," what would it be? The Empire State Building? Of course it would. There are taller things, it is true, but I am sure you will agree that nothing says "tall" with such authority, with such grace, with such imagination, as the Empire State Building.

It is 102 stories tall, and each story holds many stories, and not just a few tall tales, such as this one of Albert and Victoria, two bugs who live on the 68th floor.

That's almost 830 feet in the air, or 9,960 inches. Since neither Albert nor Victoria is much over ½ inch tall (that's $1/24$th of a foot), they are pretty hard to see. You, on the ground, wouldn't know there was a story there at all, if I didn't tell you.

Which is exactly what I am going to do.

chapter one

"My, my, my, my, my, my, MY! What a day! What a glorious day! What an unquestionably, undoubtedly, unmistakably MARVELOUS day!" Albert said out loud as he squinted into the bright sunlight, waving his antennae in all directions.

"Yes sir," he went on as he pulled first himself, then his harmonica up out of the crack he called home. "This is the life! This IS the life! A day like today makes a bug glad he's a bug!"

He stretched out his legs, one, two, three, four, five, six, and moved carefully across the jagged granite.

A breeze blew in from New Jersey. "Ah, the sea!" he said, smiling, taking a deep breath.

Albert had never been to the sea. He had never been anywhere, except the 68th floor of the Empire State Building, and he hadn't even seen all of that. Albert didn't care. Hundreds of breezes carrying thousands of smells bump into the Empire State Building every day, and Albert sniffed them all. He didn't have to see the world. The world came to him, riding the wind. It was his world, small and wide at the same time, and Albert was content.

He stuck his feet securely to the building, basking in the warm sun. The wind ruffled his coat like a tiny field of wheat, and he changed from brown to gray. He faced into the wind and, putting his harmonica to his mouth, blew a long, clear, joyful sound.

"Ah ha! There you are!" Victoria came up behind him, waving her antennae. "I've been looking everywhere for you. What are you doing?"

"Doing? What am I DOING, Victoria?" Albert turned his face to the sun and closed his eyes, a smile on his lips. "What does it look like I'm doing? What IS there for a bug to do on a wonder of a day such as this except enjoy? ENJOY!"

What was there for a bug to do, indeed. A

bug has exactly four major jobs: (1) to find a place to live; (2) to find food to eat; (3) to avoid life-stopping calamity (mainly being squashed by humans or eaten by birds); and (4) to enjoy life in the company of good, true friends. Most bugs spend their whole lives on the first three items alone, never mind number 4, scuttling here, skittering there, just trying to keep food in their stomachs and a roof over their heads. As a result, most bugs live terribly busy but nonetheless lonely lives.

This, luckily for us, was not the case for Albert and Victoria. Bug housing is plentiful on the Empire State Building, with its large number of cracks and grooves, nooks and crannies, perfect for countless bug families, large or small, rich or poor, lazy or not

Food was even easier to find. Those breezes that bump into the Empire State Building every day carry food as well as smells. Bug treats of every description—spores and fungus and worm eggs, small as dust and twice as tasty—blew in from the seashore and docks, city streets and neighborhoods, from all over the tri-state area, and were dumped daily at Albert and Victoria's doorsteps. Each morning the mats on which they wiped their sticky feet were laid out like banquet tables for royalty, fit for a queen bee.

Birds and humans? Albert and Victoria gave no second thoughts to such things.

They had never even seen a human close up, because they lived near no windows and couldn't see the people inside. They could see humans on the ground, but these, being so far away and looking so tiny, seemed to be bugs, just like themselves. They lived with no fear of squashing.

Birds did fly by, and occasionally one would turn a hungry eye on them. ("Makes my blood run colder," Albert always said.) Birds couldn't land on the side of the building, however, so they posed no real threat. Besides, it is common knowledge to all but the most desperate of birds that simple walking bugs with furry coats and sticky feet taste bad.

Not birds, not humans, not food, not shelter—no worrisome cloud crossed the sunny lives of Albert and Victoria. They were free to find each other, and, once found, they quickly became best friends.

chapter
two

Albert had known Victoria almost her whole life, and he liked her from the moment he met her. Why she was so special was something he never thought to ask himself. It would be like asking what was so special about sunlight or soft summer nights. He looked at her and he felt happy. When he was with her, it felt as if the world was a good place to be. She was his friend, he didn't ask why. That's the kind of bug Albert was.

Victoria, on the other hand, liked Albert's harmonica before she liked him. She couldn't resist a tune played truly, and she listened to him play whenever she could.

One night, Albert played and sang, *"Two of us riding nowhere..."*

It was Victoria's favorite

"...spending someone's hard-earned pay..."

She closed her eyes and swayed to the music, her antennae bobbing, keeping time.

"...Sunday driving, not arriving..."

Before she knew it, she was humming along.

Albert stopped. Victoria opened her eyes, embarrassed. "Oh, I'm sorry. Please continue—I won't do it again."

"No, no...it's not that," said Albert. "Why don't you sing?"

"Oh, I couldn't do that."

"Why not?"

"I just couldn't, that's all."

"Don't you know the words?"

"Of course I know the words. It's my favorite song. I know every one."

"Then why don't you sing them?"

Victoria looked at the ground. "Because I never sing," she blurted. "I can't sing. I have an ugly voice."

"Impossible!"

"Yes, yes, it's true." She looked up at him, her eyes widening. "Someone told me once. I have a flat, ugly voice."

"That someone must be crazy," said Albert. "Let me hear you—I'll tell you the truth, then you'll know for sure. Here we go." He raised the harmonica to his mouth.

"I can't."

Albert lowered the harmonica. "You can't if you don't try, that's true," he said. "But how can you go through life without singing? How can you go one more DAY without singing? No one will hear you but me. Don't be shy." He raised the harmonica to his mouth. "Here we go."

"Here we go," she whispered. She took a big breath and a little voice came out. *"Two of us riding nowhere..."*

Albert smiled at her and nodded his head. She sang, a little louder, *"... spending some-one's hard-earned pay."*

Albert never played better. Victoria felt the music inside her, and her voice grew bigger, bigger. Her toes tapped, her fingers snapped, her antennae beat a steady rhythm back and forth. She belted it out, *"Sunday driving, not arriving ... on our way..."*

It was an unforgettable number on a night to remember, and by the time the last strains of Albert's harmonica floated out over Manhattan, Albert and Victoria had become best friends.

Albert and Victoria were proof of an ento-mological fact: The happiest bugs in the world live on the Empire State Building. They had no chores and they had no cares and they were free all day to play and enjoy the view.

There was only one thing they had to worry about, only one fly in their ointment. But that was months away—it was nothing to worry about now.

chapter
three

Spring passed and summer passed and life was grand, filled with picnics and parties and a sky filled with fireworks on the Fourth of July. One evening, when the breezes blew just a little cooler, Albert and Victoria sat outside. Albert played on his harmonica and Victoria sang along softly, *"...you and I have memories ..."* They watched the lights of the city spread out before them like a carpet of stars.

"Oh, Albert," sighed Victoria, "it's so lovely."

"Yes, it is," he replied. "I wish it didn't have to end."

"Why does it have to end?" Victoria was a

young bug with a short memory. Why did it have to end, indeed.

"Winter. You know that," Albert explained patiently. "Summer is nice but it is only temporary. For us, living here, winter is our main season—cold, wet, windy winter. We should think about it, prepare for it, worry about it. It is a challenge just to survive, and we have to be ready."

"I don't WANT to think about it! I don't WANT to worry! It sounds awful!" Fire blazed in Victoria's eyes and she jumped to her feet. "The night is too beautiful and I am too young to think about any of that! I don't WANT to go to sleep for the whole winter. I've hardly lived yet—how can I go to sleep so soon?"

"You have no choice, Victoria. I told you before," said Albert. "That's just the way it is."

"I want to have fun and you want me to spend my youth worried, my middle age asleep, and my old age wondering what happened! The whole world can't sleep half its life away! What do birds do? What do humans do? What do bugs in Argentina do?" Victoria turned on her heels and stomped away. A creature with six feet can certainly stomp.

Albert didn't go after her. They had been through this before, and Albert could get nowhere with her.

He was worried. If a bug was careful, if he took no chances, he might be able to get through many winters, to live a long life. Victoria didn't care. "Long and boring," she called it, and she wanted no part of it. "It's not that you live longer," she told him, "it just feels like you do."

She was his best friend. She was young and beautiful, full of sparkle and life. He admired her fearless spirit. "Reckless," his friends called it, and he had to admit, her spirit terrified him, too. He watched the lights blink on below. If she didn't hibernate, if she didn't prepare, she would die. It was that simple. "What a sad thing," he thought, "to be born with a capacity for love and life the size of Elizabeth Taylor's, and to be born a bug."

A cold wind blew. "From Canada," he thought. She would have to hibernate. What else could she do? He shivered and went inside.

chapter
four

"Mama, it's not fair! Albert is just being mean! Stuffy and narrow-minded and mean!" Victoria complained to her mother. They sat outside on the patio, in the autumn sun, wrapped in dragonfly-wing shawls. It was colder than it had been, and Victoria felt sluggish and in a bad mood. They sipped evaporated hot-dog vendor water her mother had caught on a leaf, and they talked about life.

"You had better listen to Albert, child. He's right," Mama said. She looked at her daughter and shook her head. "No bug can survive the winter without hibernating, especially simple walking bugs like us. No simple walking bug has ever stayed awake through the winter and lived to tell about it. Albert is not being mean. He just wants what is best for you. He wants you to be safe."

Victoria crossed her legs and jiggled her feet. "Mama, I can't believe there isn't a way to stay awake through the winter. I HAVE been preparing for winter, in my own way. I have been collecting lint and cat fur, piece by piece. I've made hats and mufflers and leg warmers for me and for Albert. I'm preparing for winter—for winter fun! Skiing and skating and sledding—that's for me!"

Mama made a clicking sound with her ankle and drew her shawl tight around her. "Tsk, tsk—how did I ever raise such a girl?" she thought. "It must be her father's side of the family."

Just then a shadow crossed the patio, blocking out the sun. Mama and Victoria looked up, shielding their eyes with their hands. A large winged creature, black against the sky, hovered above them, sunlight glancing off his magnificent wings.

"Hiya," he said.

"Philippe!" Victoria exclaimed with de-light.

"Philippe," Mama echoed, with no delight at all.

"Vicky! My angel! What a surprise to find you here *avec** Mama, without that tiresome Albert."

Victoria blushed. "Ahem," said Mama.

"And Madame, looking more like Vicky's sister than her dear Mama"—Philippe made a small bow—"you have been well?"

"Yes, fine. Now we really should go inside, Victoria. It's getting chilly." Mama pushed back her chair.

Philippe felt the chill when he caught Mama's icy stare.

Victoria frowned. "Yes, it is getting chilly. That's the problem."

"Oh, don't you just hate the cold?" said Philippe, wrapping his wings around himself and giving a shiver. "I do. That's why I left Monte Carlo. When the cold wind blows, Philippe goes; that's my motto."

"New York is colder than Monte Carlo, Philippe. Why did you come back here?" asked Victoria.

"The holidays! To see my family! There's no place like home! And New Year's Eve wouldn't be New Year's Eve if I didn't ride that

---

**avec* (ă-vek′): French, meaning "with." Philippe liked to use French around bugs who spoke only English. It made him feel smarter than he really was.

apple down in Times Square. But January one and I'm gone to Florida. A little sun, a little golf, and I'm a new bug."

"But how can you stay here for November and December and not hibernate—or die?" Victoria was all eyes and waving antennae.

"Come along, Victoria, come inside." Mama tugged at her nervously.

"Simple, my dear. One slows down because one grows cold. One need only stay warm, and one can keep awake and dancing twelve months out of the year." He gave a small but spirited spin.

"Warm? Outside? In New York City?" She couldn't believe it.

"Warm. Outside. Right here on the Empire State Building." Philippe rubbed his hands together. "Invite me to dinner and I'll tell you how."

chapter
five

"You want me to have dinner with who?" Albert's eyes bugged out and his mouth fell open wide. He had been napping, and bits of lint and leaves stuck to his legs and antennae when he got up to answer the door.

"That's 'whom,' Albert," said Victoria, stepping inside. "Philippe. Philippe de Mothchilde. You remember him."

"Remember him? REMEMBER him??!!" Albert was wide awake now, and he paced the room, debris flying from him everywhere. "That firefly! How could I ever forget him?" he thought to himself. Out loud he said, "I thought he went away someplace. To Paris or someplace—forever."

"Monte Carlo, and he's back. I just saw him. I invited him to dinner tonight and I want you to come too."

Albert couldn't contain himself. "Oh, yeah, dinner, sure, I bet. He invited himself, didn't he? First it's dinner, then maybe a short ride on those gaudy wings of his. Before you know it, you won't have time anymore for your ordinary, dull walking friends—your life will be too full of flashy high-flyers!"

"Albert, what on earth are you talking about? It's only dinner, for goodness' sake. If I didn't know you better, I'd say you were jealous."

"Jealous!!?? ME??!! Don't make me laugh! I'm only thinking of you, Victoria. I've seen it happen, believe you me." He shook his finger at her. "Do you know how you'll end up? A dried-up old bug skin, hanging around with the irresponsible likes of him. Well, let me tell you one thing, my friend," Albert went on, working himself into a state, "you might have fun, but you won't be happy."

Albert was raving. Albert was scared. Philippe was charming. He could FLY! He had seen the sea and he had seen the world and he knew things a simple walking bug could never hope to know. How could Albert compete with that?

"Don't be ridiculous, Albert," Victoria said. "Of course, if you're too busy, or you don't want to come..."

"I'LL COME!" he almost shouted at her. He didn't want to share food with this bug, but he wanted even less for Victoria to see him alone. "It's just that...a dinner party is so much trouble, especially at this time of year. Aren't you tired? Wouldn't you rather put it off a bit— until spring, maybe?"

"Don't be silly! I feel fine! I knew I could count on you! Come early and you can help me get ready," she said cheerfully, wrapping her shawl around her. "We'll have fun, you'll see!"

"You might have fun," Albert sighed as he shut the door behind her, "but I won't be happy."

chapter
six

"Yoo-hoo! *C'est moi!*"* It was Philippe de Mothchilde at the door.

"Philippe! We're in here! Come in!" Victoria called. She had spent a frantic afternoon sweeping and polishing and scrubbing with her cat-whisker broom and bus-transfer dust-cloth. She took a bath in a dewdrop and placed a bit of iron oxide behind her antennae. It brought out the red in her eyes and she looked lovely. None of it was lost on Philippe.

"Ah, Vicky! I would have thought it impos-

C'est moi (say mwa): French, meaning "It is I," or "It's me."

sible, but you look even lovelier than you did this morning!"

Victoria blushed. Albert groaned.

Philippe had to fold his wings to get them through the door, but once inside, he flexed them flirtatiously. Albert groaned again, louder.

"Albert, old boy! I didn't see you back there! You blend right into the wall. Quite a talent, that color-change thing. Quite a talent. How have you been? How's the old kazoo?" He turned back to Victoria, without waiting for a reply.

"It's a harmonica, Philippe. I've been well—yourself?" Albert tried, for Victoria's sake, to be pleasant. She smiled at him.

"Splendid! Splendid! Just dashed up from the Statue of Liberty. It's wonderful there now. Lots of tourists leaving behind lots of lovely trash."

The city lights shone in through the doorway and lit his wings in the most dramatic way. Victoria couldn't take her eyes off them.

The evening belonged to Philippe. He told tales of daring and courage, of flying too far from land and too close to fire. He told of strange bugs in far-off lands. He made Victoria laugh often, that crystal little laugh of hers that until now Albert had loved. When she laughed,

Philippe fluttered one wing or the other, like a wink, and Albert felt worse.

It was a long evening for poor Albert. He grew sullen and moody. Is anything worse at a dinner party than being moody? Probably not. Does anything make your rival look better? Hardly.

Victoria watched Philippe over their dessert of chocolate and peanut butter she had scraped from a wrapper that blew against her doorway that morning. Finally she asked him, "Philippe, aren't you tired? It's getting so cold."

"Tired? Me? Ha! Tired is for the meek of spirit! Tired is for the cold of blood! Oh, I suppose SOME insects have to hibernate—those with no imagination. Not me! I'm not ready to spend half of my life locked away in some hole in the wall—no offense, of course."

Victoria blushed.

"Now," he continued, "if I had someone to hibernate with, it might be different...." His voice trailed off, choked with emotion. Victoria blushed harder. Albert yawned, loud and long.

"How do you do it? How do you stay awake?" she asked, after shooting Albert a dark look.

"As I started to tell you before, I stay warm."

"But how? Outside? In the winter?"

"Simple. I go up."

"Huh?" Victoria wanted very much to appear a bug of the world, but she had no idea what he was talking about.

Philippe tried to explain. "You have no energy because you are cold. You need to get warm. If you don't get warm soon, you'll sleep all the time. To get warm you have to go where it's warm, and in this neighborhood, that's up."

"Up?" She still didn't understand.

"Here, I'll show you." Philippe took her hand and led her to the doorway. Albert followed.

"Now, look up," he said.

She did. She saw the sights she saw every night—the flickering lights of buildings, an airplane or two. "You mean the lights?" she asked. It was pretty, but it was nothing new.

"Don't look out, look up. Here," he said, crouching down, "climb on my back."

"Now, just a minute!" Albert said, but Victoria was already aboard.

"Are you ready? Hold on tight," said Philippe, and he gently pushed away from the building.

"AHHHHH!" Victoria shrieked. She screwed her eyes shut and clamped every sticky foot tightly to Philippe's sides. She was in the air! She could feel Philippe's shoulders operate his heavy wings, *whoosh, whoosh.* She opened one eye and looked at the moving streams of light in the street below. Her stomach flipped over.

"Don't look down!" Philippe called back to her, too late. He beat his wings slowly, with a gentle rocking rhythm, as they hovered in the sky. For all his faults, Philippe sure could fly. Victoria calmed and opened her eyes again. What a feeling! What a wonderful, indescribable, exhilarating feeling! Freedom! She was FLYING!

"Vicky! Look up now!" Philippe called to her.

She did. "Ahhhh," she said again, not in a shriek this time, but in awe. The whole sky was lit up. It glowed as bright as day. The top of the building seemed to have been dipped in light, like a giant ice-cream cone dipped in sparkly sprinkles. What a magnificent place! Oh, to go there!

Albert stood in the doorway, helpless. There she was, his dear Victoria, in such danger, with only the bug he loathed standing between her and death, hundreds of feet below. "Victoria," he whispered.

Philippe flew back to the building and carefully touched down. Victoria slid to the

ground, every one of her knees trembling. "So that's where you're going," she said.

"Come with me," he whispered in her ear. In a louder voice he said, "Yes, all those lights keep things quite toasty up there. I leave in a few days. You, uh, I mean you BOTH, of course, are welcome to join me. Think it over. It's so much fun, just like Las Vegas."

Albert found his voice. "Why, that's out of the question! Impossible! We're walking bugs—simple walking bugs! We do not FLY! At best, we hop a bit. We can't go off gallivanting wherever the wind blows us. The wind doesn't blow us. We're walking bugs, and walking bugs stay put!"

"Whatever you say," said Philippe, looking bored. "I really must be going. Let me know if you change your mind. The dinner was lovely. Many thanks to my charming hostess." He kissed her hand.

"Good-bye, good-bye," said Albert, ushering Victoria inside. "And good riddance," he added, under his breath.

Later that night, as Victoria got ready for bed, she had a strange, faraway look in her eyes. "Las Vegas," she murmured.

chapter
seven

"I can't believe it. I can't believe you're going through with this." Albert stood in the middle of the room and twitched his antennae, the way bugs do when they don't know what to do next.

"I'm going. I don't want to discuss it anymore. I've made up my mind and I'm going." Victoria piled her things together on a leaf in the middle of the floor. She took a sesame seed from the pantry and added it to her pile. She was careful to avoid his eyes.

"Do something, Albert!" Victoria's mother sobbed. "She won't listen to me! DO something! Stop her!"

"Please, Victoria," he pleaded, "be sensible. This is crazy. You'll die if you go."

She turned to him, her eyes glistening. "And I'll die if I stay. I can't live this kind of life—your kind of life. I can't be the kind of bug you want me to be. I'm sorry, Albert. I know I've let you down. But this is my chance, maybe my only chance to see winter and see the world and live—really live! I have to take it! I have to go!" She folded the leaf over her things, binding the package together with sticky string from her feet.

Albert looked out the doorway. The sky was heavy with lead-gray clouds—a snow sky. Walking bugs weren't supposed to do this. She would never make it. Doom overtook the panic in his chest.

"Come with me."

"What?" he asked, turning toward her.

"I mean it. Come with me. I want you to. We could make it ... together. Come."

He looked at her, so brave, so sure, so full of life. He wanted to go.

"I can't."

"Yes you can!" She stamped one foot. "You say you're my friend, that you'd be lost without me—then come! For once in your life stop thinking that you can't—that you're not supposed to. You CAN!"

He couldn't go with her. He knew it the way you know things you don't have to think about. He knew it because he could feel it. Could there be more to life than friendship? Maybe so.

"Please don't ask me to go with you. If you only knew how much I wish I could. Just as you can't stay here and be happy, I can't leave. I am a walking bug—a simple walking bug. It's not much, but it is enough for me. I don't want to be anything else. I don't want to leave. I belong here, and I'd surely die if I went. As hard as it is for me to say good-bye to you, I have to. I can't go."

She looked at him for a long time. How she would miss him! "I understand," she said.

She put on her hat and her three pairs of leg warmers. She was ready.

"Oh, Victoria!" Albert ran to her and hugged her. "Please be careful out there!"

"Yoo-hoo! It's time!" It was Philippe at the door.

"Just a minute!" Victoria called. She broke away from Albert and hugged her mother. "Good-bye, Mama."

"Good-bye, my angel. Do you have everything? Will you be warm enough?" Her face was wet with tears.

"Yes, I think so. Please take care of yourself."

"Go quickly, while the weather still holds,"

said Albert. "Is it all right if I don't walk you to the door?"

"Sure...well, I guess this is it, then...."

"Do you think you'll ever come back?"

"Of course! In the spring! You'll be just waking up—you won't even know I was gone!" Both laughed, but neither believed it.

"Don't forget me, okay?" she asked, standing in the doorway, her bundle under her arm.

"I'll never forget you, Victoria," he said, his voice cracking.

"Vicky! Vicky! Time waits for no bug! Shake some legs!" Philippe called, impatiently.

"Okay, okay," she called. "Look after Mama for me, will you?"

"Sure."

"Be happy, okay?"

"Of course."

"Promise?"

"Anything for you."

She tossed her muffler over her shoulder as she went out the door. Albert waited a minute, then ran to the doorway, just in time to watch her and Philippe rise up into the sky, into the gray. He watched them until they disappeared.

He had forgotten to tell her that he loved her.

chapter
eight

"Well now, that's that," Albert thought as he arrived home, shutting his door behind him. He slapped his hands together as if removing chalky dust. He was determined not to be melancholy. He was determined not to be sad.

"She made her decision, I made mine, now life goes on," he said, talking to himself out loud now. "I won't think about her. I won't think about her at all. After all, isn't this the moment I've been waiting for? What joy, what freedom, to be able to hibernate at will, without someone whining at me to stay awake! Ah! Here we go!"

He put an extra armful of leaves on his bed and hopped into it, snuggling down inside all warm and cozy. "Mmmmm," he said. "How marvelous! I'm off to dreamland, without another thought for Victoria!"

He closed his eyes.

He opened his eyes.

He plumped some lint under his head. "Once I fall asleep, I won't think about her anymore," he said. He flipped over on his side.

He closed his eyes.

He opened his eyes.

"Maybe I'll dream about her," he thought. He flipped onto his back, and crossed four arms over his abdomen.

He closed his eyes.

They popped open again. He couldn't do it. He couldn't fall asleep. He had been dragging himself around, waiting for this moment for a month, and now that it was here, he couldn't do it. He kept thinking about Victoria. He missed her.

He tried everything. He added lint to his leaves to make his bed softer. He put a piece of ice-cream stick under his bed to make it harder. He moved his bed closer to the door to get some fresh air. He did 15 deep knee bends for each set of knees and brewed himself a cup of air vent tea. He paged through scraps of old *New York Times* editorials. Nothing worked. He was wide awake and full of worry.

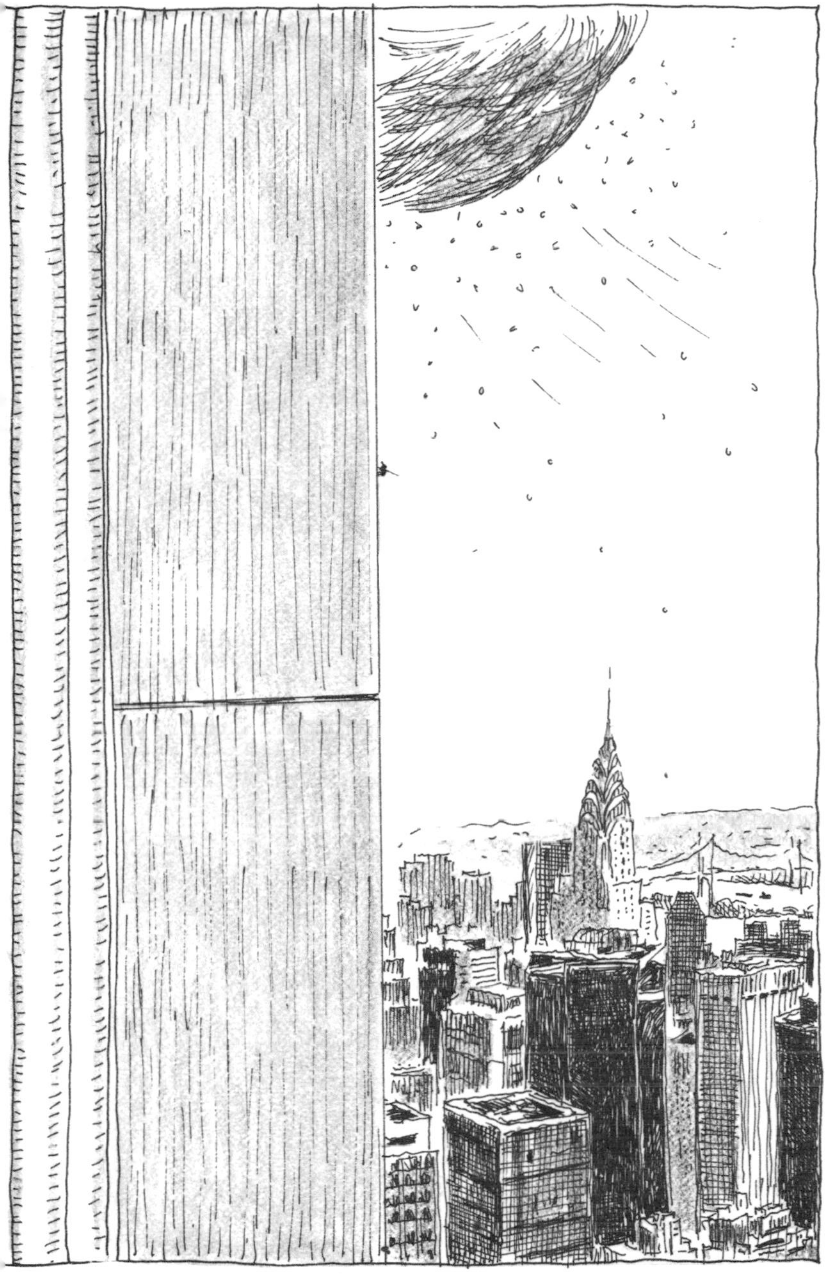

"Is she alive? Is she happy? Does she laugh at his jokes?" These thoughts and a hundred more kept racing through his head. He sat up and took his harmonica from under his pillow. He played thoughtfully, *"...And when the brokenhearted people..."*

It came to him slowly, what he must do, as he lay there on his bed in the lengthening gloom of the oncoming winter. Why hadn't he realized it before? Was it pride? Anger? Stubbornness? Maybe there was more to life than friendship, but what was life without it, without some bug to be with, to share with, to care about? A life like that felt like nothing. It felt worse than nothing—it felt bad. A life like that wasn't worth living, asleep or awake.

"...There will be an answer..." It was clear. Life without her would be worse than the calamity that was sure to befall him if he went after her.

"I'll do it," he said, throwing off his leaves and jumping from his bed. "I'll go."

To make a decision, even such a crazy one, filled him with purpose. At least he had a plan of action, and, "Everyone needs a plan of action, as my Aunt Ant used to say," said Albert. He went to the doorway and looked outside. "It doesn't look bad, not bad at all. I might even make it!" he said.

He quickly prepared for the journey, gathering together a few belongings and all the food he could carry, for there would certainly be no insect eateries open along the way. "Not at this time of year," he thought, with a shudder. He put on his hat and muffler and all six leg warmers. He took his toothpick-splinter walking stick from the front hall and hoisted his pack onto his back, his harmonica tied carefully to the top. He took a final look around. Would he ever see his dear little cubbyhole again? "Mustn't think like that," he thought. "Only positive thoughts will get me to the top." He strode to the door, full of hope and a little fear. He took a deep breath and plunged outside.

"Well then," he said, "up we go!"

chapter
nine

The trip didn't take long, but to Victoria it seemed like hours. It is a scientific fact that distance seems longer the smaller you are. It didn't help that Philippe didn't fly directly there. Moths aren't like that. They flutter a little this way, then that way a little. The expression is "as the crow flies" and not "as the moth flies" for exactly this reason.

It was windy, too. They would fly a little to the left, the wind would blow them twice as far to the right, when all they really wanted to do was go straight up the middle. Between the fluttering here and the blowing there, it was a very bumpy flight.

It was cold, too—so cold that Victoria grew

numb. She couldn't feel anything. The only reason she held on to Philippe was because she froze in that position. The only reason she knew she was alive was because she wanted to throw up. Where there was nausea, there was hope.

And it snowed, right before they reached their destination. It was a driving, blinding, sudden snow with fat, wet snowflakes, each one bigger than Philippe and Victoria together. Philippe tried to fly between them, but he couldn't dodge them all. SPLAT! They were hit with a wet, sloppy flake. Philippe gasped and faltered, but he kept moving. Victoria was wet, soaked to her exoskeleton. She buried her face against Philippe's back. "Skiing? Skating? Sledding? In weather like this? Ugh!" she thought.

At last they arrived. They lit on a gray slab. It was all gray to Victoria—the ground, the sky, the mist that hung heavily around them. Her head ached, she felt woozy, her legs were so numb she fell rather than climbed from Philippe's back. "Where are all the lights?" she asked.

"Soon, sweetie, soon," said Philippe, stretching his back and his legs. "It's almost time. Don't you worry. You'll warm up then. A little heat, a little rest, and you'll be a new bug."

"Philippe! Philippe, my man! It's about time! I was beginning to think you weren't going to make it this year! And who is this?" Philippe's friend Jocko glided up to them smoothly and landed neatly, with obvious style.

"That's Vicky, from the old neighborhood. She has never been to the top before—said I'd give her a lift. Vicky, Jocko. Jocko, Vicky," he made introductions.

"Charmed. Hey, you don't look so good," said Jocko.

"I don't feel so good," said Victoria. She had never seen a bug wear sunglasses before.

"Oh, she's not used to flying," said Philippe. "She's not used to the cold. She's not used to a lot of things. But that's all going to change. Right, love? We're going to show her a few sights, a little fun—it will be a whole new life for her. But first, she has to recover. Here, give me a hand. This spotlight should warm her up."

Philippe and Jocko placed Victoria just under the rim of an enormous spotlight and tucked her muffler in around her. "Rest here," said Philippe, placing her bundle under her head as a pillow. "I'm going to see some bugs, get a little dinner. I'll bring something back."

Victoria's eyes were closing as he spoke. The sleep she had been avoiding for so long came, and it was welcome.

chapter
ten

"Onetwothreefourfivesix, onetwothreefourfive-six," Albert counted as he marched along. It was easier than he had expected it to be. In his hat and leg warmers and muffler he laughed at the cold. As long as he didn't think about it, he didn't mind the wind a bit. The day was crisp and the smell of chestnuts roasting reached him from the street below. In spite of his fear, Albert felt a little thrill of adventure sneak into his soul. "What a trailblazer!" he almost shouted, waving his walking stick in the air. "What a pioneer! Walking bugs for generations to come will tell their children—their GRAND-children about me!" This thought pleased him and put a bounce in his step.

He walked on. And on. He kept to the right of a strip of metal that went up the side of the building. "I'll follow this straight to the top," he said to himself. He talked out loud for company. "Traveling is not so bad. Why have walking bugs been so against it for so many years?"

He walked on. And on. "Traveling isn't bad at all," he said, "except for the fact that there is so much walking involved."

He walked on.

"And it's lonely."

And on.

"And boring."

When you are very small, the scenery changes slowly.

He had gone up four slabs—across the slab, down into the groove between slabs, across the groove, up the side of the groove, onto the next slab, across the slab, over and over four times. He had gone farther than he had since the days of his youth, before he knew Victoria. There was no one around and he was all alone.

He was about to climb down into the next groove, when it wiggled. Albert pulled his foot back, and studied the crack and its contents. A broad smile broke out on his face.

"Well, I'll be! If it isn't Miss Cornelia! Miss Cornelia P. Worm!" he said to the worm's middle. He was never quite sure which end

was up with Miss Cornelia. One end raised itself out of the crack and waved in his direction. She couldn't see very well, but she had an excellent sense of hearing. She was Albert's music teacher from second grade.

"Albert, is that you?"

"Yes, Miss Cornelia, it's Albert. How are you?" He was so pleased to run into someone he knew, in such a forlorn place. He hunched down to have a chat.

"Can't talk now, Albert. I have to finish my winter digs. It seems like each year I move a little more slowly. Have to hurry—winter's coming. Why are you not home asleep? Don't you realize how late it is, young man?" As she spoke she dug into the dirt, loosening the soil a little more with each word.

"I'm not hibernating this year, Miss Cornelia. I'm having an adventure. I'm..."

"Not hibernating? Have you lost your senses? Do you see how thick my middle is? Do you know what that means? That means we're in for a bad winter, Albert, very bad. Young people today... well, you'll never make it, son, never make it. You'll never amount to anything..." With that, most of her slipped beneath the dirt's surface, leaving only her nontalking end in sight.

"Well, thank yoooou," Albert said to the

little pointed tail. "Boy," he muttered, getting up and brushing the dirt from his leg warmers. He was in a bad mood now, very bad. "She was that way in school, too," he remembered.

He tried to shake off the bad feeling from his meeting with Miss Cornelia. "Musn't think about it," he said. "Only positive thoughts will get me through. One, two, three, four, five, six."

He was in unfamiliar territory now, and the slabs were deserted. He was alone again, and there was no sound. He could hear the wind and the clatter of the traffic below, but that familiar undertow of sound, the constant bath of humming, buzzing bug vibrations in which he lived—which is always there when bugs are about, which tells bugs they are one of a family and the earth is a friendly place—was silent. He kept on. "One, two, three. One, two, three."

It got darker and colder and it was time to make camp for the night. "This looks like a good place," he thought, as he climbed down into an especially dusty groove. He untied his bundle and spread the leaf over the top to serve as a roof. He secured the edges with goop from his feet and piled his belongings around himself to cut out the wind.

It was a fine camp, and cozy, and Albert's mood brightened as he admired his work. "Albert, you amaze me," he said to himself as he stood with his hands on his hips. "One day you're living in the lap of bug luxury, and the next, here you are, in the wilderness, where it's survival of the fittest."

He looked down and patted his paunch. He feasted on bread crumbs and played a vagabond tune on his harmonica. *"The long and winding road..."* floated up out of the groove and into the night air.

He checked the position of the metal strip outside so he'd be sure to travel in the right direction in the morning. He scooped out a shallow trench in the groove and wrapped his muffler around himself. With dust for a blanket, he settled down to sleep. As he was drifting off, Miss Cornelia's words filled his head: "You'll never make it. You'll never make it."

"You're wrong, Miss Cornelia," Albert said out into the darkness. "You said I'd never learn to play the harmonica and you were wrong about that—you're wrong about this, too. I WILL make it. I'll find Victoria and I'll get to the top. I will, I will...," he repeated until he was fast asleep.

chapter
eleven

"Where am I?" Victoria opened her eyes. It was so unfamiliar. "Did I hibernate after all? It's so warm!" She sat up. "And so bright!" She dangled her legs over the silvery edge of the lamp and shaded her eyes with her hand.

She remembered. "The top!" Another spotlight, just like hers, sat across the way, and together they lit up the sky. They formed a golden cradle of light, bright and warm. It was dark and cold beyond, and she could see snowflakes falling against the black sky. But there, in the circle of light, Victoria felt warm and safe.

When her eyes adjusted to the light, Victoria saw that there were snowflakes falling within the light, too. "How can that be?" she wondered. "Why don't they melt?" Then she realized that they were not snowflakes at all, but bugs, hundreds of flying bugs, swirling and spinning and sparkling like diamonds, in gowns of silver, on wings of silk. How fine they were! How light! How quick! The lamps hummed the melody, their many wings beat the harmony, and they danced, singly and in pairs and in bunches, bunches of bugs.

"If only Albert could see this!" thought Victoria, clapping her hands. She started tapping her toes in time to the music. Their stickiness made little sucking noises on the edge of the lamp. She stopped and looked quickly around, embarrassed. Had anyone heard? She wouldn't have cared about it if Albert were there.

Albert. She thought back to that first time he got her to sing. "If Albert were here, he wouldn't care if our feet made noise. We'd dance anyway!" She took a few cha-cha steps, thinking of him. The goop on her feet slowed her down. "If only I could fly!" she thought. "Where is Philippe, anyway?"

"So, you've finally come to, have you?" Philippe hovered just above her head in a cloud of bugs, all laughing and giggling. Had they been watching her?

She felt her cheeks grow warm. "I'm sorry. I must have been more tired than I thought."

"The night is young, and the best is yet to come," said Philippe, with a praying mantis under each wing. "Jocko is throwing a party on that light over there. He found a piece of chocolate turtle in front of Macy's yesterday. Want to come? A few laughs, a little dancing—it will be fun!"

She looked at them. They were all so beautiful, with sleek little heads and long graceful legs and wings, those wings! She looked so different, her round head stuck with antennae, and thick, sturdy legs. She looked at their feet—narrow, slender. She looked down at her own sensible, sticky feet, designed to stay put, not to dance on air.

"I'm still pretty tired, Philippe. Do you mind if I stay here?"

"Of course not, my sweet, whatever you wish. See you later!" Philippe and his friends rose up into the air in a single mass and blew away like a puff of dust.

He hadn't even tried to talk her into going.

chapter
twelve

Albert woke to a terrible storm. The wind cut under his leaf and ripped one side free from the granite. It flapped over his head.

"Uh oh," he thought. "Just when things were going so well. That is, just when things weren't going too badly." He peeked his head up out of the groove. It was snowy and windy and he couldn't see very far. He could barely make out his guiding strip of metal, just a short distance away.

"Now, don't panic," he told himself as he sank back into the dust, fighting the panic in his chest. "Think, think. What are your choices?"

Absently he reached for his harmonica. *"And in my hour of darkness..."*

"One: I can stay here. No, I can't. The groove is too shallow and I'd freeze in no time. Okay. Two: I could find one of those sealed-up cracks I passed along the way and try to wake the bugs inside—take refuge with the kindness of strangers. No, I can't do that. Even if I could make them hear me, which I doubt, they might not have enough food for the winter for me, too. No, I can't endanger the lives of my fellow bugs. Well then, three: I could turn back."

The thought of his warm little nest, filled with food and a comfortable bed, made his throat ache. Then he thought of Victoria. He figured he was about halfway between Victoria and his home. In one direction was merely food and shelter and safety. In the other was the best friend he ever had.

"When you put it that way, Albert, old boy," he said to himself, "there's really no choice at all." He took another look at the storm. "A passing squall! It will blow over in no time. Then, onward and upward!"

His jaw trembled and he put his harmonica to his mouth. "... *There will be an answer...*" He sounded fine. "I'll make it," he thought.

Actually, his chances of making it were very, very slim.

chapter thirteen

"What? Going out again tonight?" Victoria snapped as she watched Philippe prepare for another evening of social whirling and twirling, in the mirrored surface of the spotlight's edge. Philippe straightened his necktie and pretended not to hear.

"What's wrong with everybody, anyway?" Victoria thought to herself. Victoria had been at the top for almost a week, and it was not at all what she expected it to be.

Sure, bugs danced all night, but they had to sleep all day just to get through the cold, overcast hours until the lights came on. Once they did, the bugs were trapped within the warm circle of their glow.

A party is fun and then you go home,

right? Imagine a party that never ended, and you couldn't go home even if you wanted to. Can you imagine dancing every night, night after night, whether you wanted to or not?

Victoria was too shy to dance much. She had no wings and her sticky feet made noise. She sat out most of the dances and she sat alone most of the time. You can't make many friends if you're always dancing. You can't make ANY friends if everyone is dancing and you are not.

Victoria was not a happy bug. She was not having any fun, either.

She dangled her feet over the light and watched Philippe. "Where I come from, we do things differently. We don't flit around everywhere all year long. We don't float all over the place like bubbles in champagne."

Philippe touched some cologne to where his hairline would be, if he had hair. He continued to ignore her.

"We're deep, where I come from. We're intellectual. We think. We feel."

"You whine! You nag!" Philippe slammed down his clothes brush and turned to face her. *"Les carottes sont cuites!"** he yelled at her.

Les carottes sont cuites! (lay ka-rot' soan kweet): *French,* literal translation: "The carrots are cooked!" meaning "I've had it!"

"I just don't get it. You were so full of fun before, so full of adventure. But ever since you've come here you've been moody, unfriendly, a real pain in the stinger. I hate to say it, Victoria, but you've turned into a real bore!"

Victoria felt as if she had been slapped. Whining? Nagging? A BORE?!! "I am not!" she whined. "Everyone is mean to me!"

"MEAN to you? I think you mean that bugs here don't pamper you like that mealybug Albert you're always talking about."

"Don't call Albert names."

"You compare everything here to the 68th floor. You compare everyone here to Albert. Have you TRIED to like it here? Have you TRIED to be a friend, a REAL friend to anyone? NO! You don't know how to be a friend! No wonder no one likes you here. Albert is supposed to be your great friend, and look how you treated him. Did you stop for one minute to think of his feelings? No! You only think of yourself. You feel sorry for yourself all the time. You're miserable all the time. You're no fun, Vicky. What good are you if you're no fun?"

"But that kind of fun..."

"What do you want? You're not asleep, are you? Isn't that what you wanted? There are parties every night and charming, glamorous bugs all around you—isn't that what you wanted?"

"Yes, but I thought . . ."

"If Albert is so important to you and everything was so wonderful before, just WHY did you come here?" With that, Philippe spun on his polished patent leather heel and flew away.

Why had she come? Philippe was a shallow cockroach, she saw that now, but there was truth in what he said. She had wanted fun, excitement, glamour. Now she was surrounded by all of that, and she still wasn't happy.

She was lonely. She was surrounded by thousands of bugs, and she was lonely. It wasn't a dancing partner she was lonely for. She was lonely for someone to walk with, to talk with, to sit and look at the stars with. She was lonely for someone to tell her secrets to, for someone to tell her jokes to, for someone who believed in her and liked her just the way she was.

Albert.

Philippe was right, she had treated Albert badly. She thought she wanted fun more than she wanted him, but now she saw that nothing was as much fun without him. The truth hit her, and she said to herself, "It's the bug, not the place, that's important."

Albert had been a good friend to her, the

kind you don't run into every day. Didn't he get her to sing again? Hadn't he let her run off to the top, without much of an argument, because he knew it was something she had to do? It broke his heart—she realized that now—but did that matter to her at the time?

"No," she said, bitterly and out loud. "And now I've lost him, and I've ruined everything. I'll never get the chance to tell him what he means to me, to show him that I've changed and I do care about his feelings." She collapsed on the spotlight in a heaving sea of tears. "If only I could tell him," she sobbed. "If only I could tell him how much I miss him."

Her legs hung limp in front of the light, sending dark shapes out against the cloudy night sky. "Hold on," she said. She stopped crying and lifted her head, her brain racing with the beginnings of a brilliant idea. "Maybe there IS a way... no, he's asleep, he'd never see it. But what if he's not asleep? What if he CAN'T sleep? What if he's miserable, like I am, and right now he's standing in his doorway, looking out at this same sky? It's a small chance, but I have to take it!"

She smeared goop from her feet onto the surface of the lamp. The light shone out into the mist, a dark spot showing where the goop was smeared.

"Perfect," she said. She put on the sun-glasses Jocko had left behind, and she hopped onto the face of the light. The hot surface made the stickiness of her feet flow freely, and she skated across the bright smoothness, leaving a very important message in her wake.

chapter fourteen

Albert had no idea how long he had been walking. He couldn't tell if it was light or dark, day or night. He was bent against the wind, his head down, his eyes on the gray, and by sheer will he forced his ragged body on. "One. Two. One. Two." For every three steps he took forward the wind blew him back two, and progress was slow. He ached and all he wished for was sleep. But he dared not stop. It is when the going is hardest that victory is lost or won. To stop was never to see Victoria again. To stop was to die.

Just then he heard a noise from above, a noise different from the wind, a flapping, a fluttering. WHOOSH! Albert stopped, petrified. Something had passed by, so close it almost knocked him off his feet.

"Oh no!" he cried when he spotted it. A bird, desperate with hunger and blown off course by the storm, had seen him. She circled a short distance away, her dirty white wings spread wide, gliding with grim determination.

Albert watched as the bird made a graceful arc, and turned to face him. He looked into the gull's shiny black eyes—no chance of mercy there. "She wants to eat me," thought Albert, and fear pushed all the numbness away. What could he do? There was no place to go, and he was defenseless. The bird launched her attack. Albert didn't run. If this was it, he wanted to meet his end with honor.

WHOOSH! The bird struck, but missed him with her great beak. "AHHHH!" Albert screamed as he was knocked on his back and slid down the face of the building.

He bumped to a stop inside a groove, held fast by the sticky string binding his backpack. He was more vulnerable than ever, his legs all useless and waving in the air, his tender belly exposed to that terrible beast. Albert frantically twitched his head this way and that, searching for the bird. He jerked his head around. Where was she?

Then he saw it. There, written across a cloud, as big as the sky: ALBERT, IT'S NO FUN WITHOUT YOU.

Where had that come from? It didn't matter. Victoria missed him! He had to see her! He couldn't die now!

He didn't know how, but the strength of a thousand bugs surged through Albert. He had to survive. He spotted the bird making her turn, coming in for the kill. As she approached, Albert got ready. Flap, flap, evenly, smoothly, the bird kept coming. He looked the bird in the eye, steely eye to steely eye. He was ready for her. She opened her beak.

"Take that, you feathered fiend!" Albert

plunged his walking stick deep within the bird's down, to prick the skin beneath.

"AWK!" the bird screeched, missing Albert with her beak. She beat her wings and backed away, eyeing him. This bug had bite, but that wouldn't stop her.

"Oh, a fight to the finish, is it?" Albert said when he saw her about to return. "Well, come on, birdie, I'm ready for you." With a power he had no idea he had, he tightened his grip on his stick, ready for the bird's attack.

"AWK!" the bird screamed as Albert struck at her again, driving her back a second time.

"Forget it," Albert shouted at her, "I won't be your dinner today!" He watched as the bird watched him, every fiber of his being taut and ready.

She studied him as she flew slowly around him. She had never come up against an armed bug before. If only she wasn't so hungry...

Just then something caught her eye farther down on the building—something Albert couldn't see. Albert watched as the bird plunged down, out of sight. That made him more nervous than ever. What was she up to?

"AHHHH! AHHHH! HELP ME! HELP MEEE!!!" Albert heard screams, a familiar voice. "It can't be! I know that bug!"

He looked up to see the bird fly by with a fat green worm in her beak. "Miss Cornelia!"

The bird circled once, smugly, as if to say, "Who needs a bitter old walking bug when there are juicy worms to be had?" Then she tilted her head back and slurped Miss Cornelia down, right in front of Albert. He looked for a moment into the worm's astonished eyes, and then she was gone.

"Oh, yuck!" he said. Life can be cruel on the Empire State Building.

"Poor Miss Cornelia. I guess she didn't cover her tail." Albert shook his head. A bug never likes to see a bug get eaten, even an unfriendly, know-it-all bug like Miss Cornelia. "She saved my life," thought Albert, and he

was silent for a moment in tribute and grati-
tude.

Then the thought of the bird's possible
return urged him on. "On to Victoria!" he said.
"No time to lose." He stuck his three feet
securely to the building. Giving a mighty
heave, he flipped himself over. He slapped the
dust from his first two hands, and rescued his
harmonica, wedged into the groove. *"Toot!"* It
was slightly dented, but it still sounded fine.

He pushed his hat down on his head. "It
can't be too much farther." He picked up a tiny
feather the bird had dropped, and stuck it in
his cap. "Victoria, sweetie, I'm on my way!"

epilogue

"Victoria!" Albert called as he pulled himself up over the edge of the light.

He made it! You knew he would, didn't you?

"Albert!" she cried. She had been sitting there, wishing she could see him again, and presto! There he was!

It was a marvelous reunion, with much bug hugging and laughing and hugging again. She told him all about her idea to send a message to him across the sky, and he was certain he had never met a more clever bug. He told her all about his bravery in the face of death and disaster, and she was proud. He told his tale of adventure and Miss Cornelia's gruesome demise, and even the flying bugs stopped to listen. Then they all hugged each other, glad that they were safe. Albert just had to play, *"...we're on our way home..."* out of sheer celebration, and Victoria sang along. Everyone danced and had a good time, and Victoria heard one of the flying bugs say, "She's not such a bad gnat after all."

They never did go back down. They made friends with the flying bugs, and they discovered a colony of walking bugs tucked amidst the lights. They weren't as flashy as the flying bugs, but they had keen wit and were nice all the same.

They went back in the summer to visit Mama, but they made their life at the top a good place for a fresh start. They both changed, entirely for the better. Albert added a little fun to his worry, and Victoria added a little worry to her fun. They didn't hibernate, but they took naps.

They spent each day, every day, trying to be true friends to each other, and in the process they led very happy lives. They danced, too, but in their own way—on the ground, not in the air, and to their own music, ever after.